ALL ROADS LEAD TO HELL

MALLORY STORM

Cover and illustrations by
Robert Gibson Jones

From Mammoth Western • December 1950
Reformatted and edited by Raven's Head Press

ISBN-13: 978-0692688410 ISBN-10: 0692688412

Raven's Head Press
ravenheadpress.com

RAVEN'S HEAD
PRESS

NEVER SAY NEVERMORE

WATE McCORD was a man who lived for a dream. For two long months he'd lived for it and with it. Now, rolled in his blanket under the stars, the dream was torturing him again. He writhed, muttered to himself, and clawed at the hard ground with stiff fingers. A few drops of sweat appeared on his fore- head. But he slept on, reliving asleep what had once been reality....

"Let's walk out past the grove," Candy had said. Candy had some‐ thing in her voice that always made Wate tingle inside. She was brown as a berry‐Candy Thompson‐with rich honey-colored hair, and a slim body as straight as a sky-line pine. Wate always felt clumsy, foolishly tongue-tied when Candy was near him.

"And that gun," she said. "Must you carry it everywhere with you? What does a Kansas farmer need of a gun all the time?"

"You know as well as I do," Wate replied. "The raiders are getting worse. They cleaned out three farms over east the other night. Took twenty-five head of horses, and burned Frank Leland's barn. They cut up Frank, so maybe he won't live. A man's even afraid to leave his place for a trip to the neighbors.... "

Candy was teasing him. Using her wiles because she knew how she affected Wate. Mischievously enough, but still using them: "Are you even afraid to ride three miles to court a girl, darling? I think I'm hurt."

He reached out a clumsy hand. "You know I'd travel halfway around the world to–"

She laughed, avoided his grasp and danced away, "Leave it here in your buggy. The gun, I mean. A girl doesn't like to be made love to with a big piece of iron poking her in the ribs."

Wate grinned, put the .45 Colt under the cushion of the front seat, and followed the running Candy at an ungainly lope.

By the side of the grove, she stopped. She turned and raised her face to his. Then, she was in Wate's arms and he found that her body was trembling. They kissed each other.

Candy's voice was a choked whisper as she pressed in against Wate's big body, offered herself unreservedly to the man she loved.

"Oh, Wate– darling! I want you so badly– want you so! Must we keep on waiting...waiting..."

He laughed softly, giddy with happiness. "It's only been six months, baby. After all, there are the conventions, certain motions we have to go through."

She finished bruising his lip with her sharp white teeth and said fiercely, "Conventions be damned! I love you– love you– love you– you big stupid peasant. I want to start having your children, and I don't want to waste any time!"

"Well, now, if that ain't as pretty a picture as you'd ever get a chance to see."

The voice came seemingly from nowhere, to send cold shock

through the bodies of the two lovers. They were jerked instantly back to the place and the time. The four men had come up quietly, all carrying six- guns that glinted in the moonlight.

The speaker towered over the other three, and as Candy broke from Wate's arms, this giant ruffian had eyes only for the girl. "As nice a filly as I've seen in miles around," he told his companions. "Tell me, any of you ever see a nicer built gal?"

Wate came unfroze now. He thrust Candy behind him. "What is this?" He tried to speak quietly, but his voice was a yell. "Who are you?" he demanded.

"The name's Queen—Bill Queen," the big man said, without taking his eyes from Candy. Then, he made a quick motion with his hand as he stepped forward, and his three underlings went into action.

They knew their business, these three. They converged on Wate from different directions, moving in with fist, gun butt, and boot. Wate struck out twice, finding flesh and bone each time. But he never had a chance, because he was stunned immediately by a gun butt at the base of his skull, and then he was only half a man fighting a futile battle.

A kick in the groin doubled him up, and he lay horseshoed on the ground as another kick at the base of his spine straightened him out into writhing impotence.

But he scarcely felt the pain, so great was the agony in his mind. Consciousness remained clear and bright within him, but his body would not respond to commands from the brain; his feet and arms ignored the command: Get up and fight! Get up and fight!

So he lay helpless watching the man who called himself Queen lay hands on Candy. Here was an agony Wate would never forget. Candy had not tried to flee. Evidently she, too, had been numbed by surprise. When she did recover, it was too late.

Then, there were the things which made Wate's dream a thing of sheer horror: Queen holding Candy helpless with one great hand while his other hand explored—Candy's outraged scream as he jerked her billowing skirt high for the edification of the other three.

He lay helpless watching the man who called himself Queen lay hands on Candy.

"What'd I tell you," Candy laughed. "Ever see a nicer filly than that? And just ripe for—"

It was that last word that always brought Wate, trembling and sweat-soaked, out of his dream. He awoke now, to find his blanket had been kicked away and that his horse, on tether in the grass nearby, was snorting and pawing the ground.

He arose to a sitting position and laid his forehead on his knees. His voice was thick, weary, as he said, "Easy, boy. It's all right. Everything's all right."

But it was not all right for Wate McCord. After the dream came—bringing the picture of the past—he could never refrain from torturing himself in his mind. Always his memory was ready to take on where the dream stopped.

Bill Queen picking Candy up like a doll and forking her into the saddle of his horse, the big man mounting behind her. The last things Wate saw before the crushing blow of a gun-butt brought darkness were Candy's terrified eyes above the hand Queen held over her mouth—Candy's slim, naked legs kicking, twisting, fighting, but to no avail. Then came the thudding blow, which sent Wate into the land of dark, smothering oblivion.

He remembered coming to and staggering back to the Thompson farmhouse to find John Thompson bloody and insensible, with his wife crouching over him in sheer terror. The stock was gone, the barn in flames.

The raiders had passed through.

For hours, Wate, lantern in hand, searched the surrounding area expecting each moment to come upon Candy's ravished body. Dawn came, and he continued to search until he could tell the bandaged John Thompson, with entire certainty, "They took her with them. God knows what else happened, but one thing's sure: Candy is with Bill Queen, and I've been six kinds of a fool."

The Thompsons were still in a state of shock. They faced this new reality because they were alive and must face it, but it was glazed over, and they saw it as through a twisted mirror.

"Why a fool, Wate?" Jenny Thompson asked weakly. "You did your best."

"Not my best. Instead of hunting for Candy, I should have taken out after them. Now, they've vanished.

"I'll find Queen, of course, but it will be too late to do Candy any good. I did the wrong thing. A man should Did Hawkins give you a fair price?" train himself to do the right thing."

John Thompson laid a hand on Wate's shoulder and saw something that he had not seen before: The iciness in the gray eyes, the dark harsh lines around the mouth, the mask of bitterness which would remain forever. The face of a Kansas farmer turned overnight into a killer.

Jenny Thompson saw these things, too. And out of her own anguish, she found words: "Don't take it so hard, Wate. Now's the time we find the stuff we're made of, son. In times like these, a body has to live by his own strength. It isn't going to help Candy any if we go to pieces."

Wate looked at her grimly. "I'm not going to pieces, Mother Thompson. Not by a long shot."

Next day, Sheriff Warner found Wate, saddled and gunned, leading his six horses, on a line, out of his barnyard. Warner was a lean, hawk-faced man with handlebar mustaches and a six-gun worn high on his hip.

"Heard you sold out, McCord. Dumped the whole thing lock, stock and barrel?"

Wate's expression did not change. "Any word? Any sign of them?"

Warner shook his head. He seemed sad, and a trifle bewildered. "Not hide nor hair. They went south like grease through a hot horn, taking the horses and the Thompson girl with them. First case of outright kidnapping I've heard of, so I got a hunch they'll keep moving 'til maybe they hit the Nations, or some other place where they're safe."

"Even hell isn't safe for Queen," Wate said. "He can't ride a road I won't follow."

"Most roads lead to hell these days, it seems like," Warner said. "Heard the bank took over your place, Wate. Did Hawkins give you a fair price?"

"Fair enough. Sold the horses to John Thompson laid a hand on Peterson down the road. I'm delivering them now."

"And then?"

"I'm taking a ride—a long ride."

The lawman twisted in his saddle, an uneasiness in his manner. "Son, I know you've had a hard bump, and I'm not one to throw advice around, but don't you think you ought to stay put and let the law handle this?"

"The law? What law? I haven't seen any around here lately."

Warner reddened. "You've got to give us a chance. In a way, the Civil War's still being fought out here. All these renegades and blacklegs are using unsettled times and sectional feeling as excuses to run riot. We'll get the, though. We'll put them down."

"What's that got to do with me?" Wate asked coldly.

"I know how you feel, boy, but you were doing so well. You're a farmer, by nature. What chance you got down among those thieves and murderers? Why, you can't even use a gun."

"No? Maybe you'd be surprised, Sheriff. I've had a lot of time out here, and it so happens I made guns my hobby. It was just for fun when I did it, but I'm mighty glad now."

With that, Wate's right hand moved. There were four explosions of a gun fired upward at an angle from the hip. Then, the gun was holstered again almost before Warner had seen it drawn.

The sheriff stared in silence. There were four lightning rods protruding upward from the four corners of the barn. Until now, each rod had had an ornamental knob on its tip. The ornamental knobs were gone now, and Wate was saying, "Tell Hawkins at the bank that those knobs were only decoration, anyhow. So long, sheriff. Happy hunting." And Wate McCord went down the road to the south, leading his horses behind him.

Warner watched until he was out of sight, then turned his own mount back toward town, muttering the while, "I can see his point. Losing a girl like Candy Thompson would be mighty hard to take, but he should still ought to let the law handle them things."

9

In the beginning, it had seemed both insane and maddening to Wate that he could not come upon Bill Queen in a matter of days or, at least, weeks. Then, it dawned upon him what an immense country he lived in; what tremendous stretches of land lay in all directions to an ever-receding horizon. And he came to know what a tiny, antlike thing a man was, crawling across these limitless areas searching for another man. One who seemed to have utterly vanished.

No one had seen Bill Queen down there in the Nations. Criminals all, the inhabitants of that infamous strip were banded together in a league of silence. Then, the first touch of luck. A spot in the desert far out beyond law and order. A few adobes. A Mexican behind a counter on which sat several bottles and jugs.

"*Buenas dias*, Senor. You are thirsty, no? Is good wine. Good wheesky."

"I'm thirsty, yes." Wate poured whiskey into a dirty tumbler and lifted it to his lips.

The Mexican had long greasy hair that partially covered a knife-scar running livid across his forehead. He had an evil mouth full of rotten teeth, and he held out a restraining hand that almost touched Wate, but not quite.

"You have gold, Senor? Gold, or you do not drink. Bills, pah! Paper is of no use."

Wate lowered the glass slowly, not looking much like a Kansas farmer. His hand went across the counter, got the Mexican by the shirt-front and hauled him forward. His other hand slapped hard on either side of the dark face. Then, he hurled the man backward against the wall and watched him drip to the floor like a handful of wet mud.

"I have gold, yes," Wate told him mildly.

The Mexican smiled under Wate's cold eyes. He did not move as Wate lifted the tumbler and drained it— a fistful of raw whisky—in three gulps.

The Mexican got slowly to his feet, stepped to the counter, and stared with unblinking eyes at the hand in which Wate now held gold pieces, the number of which the Mexican could not ascertain.

Wate dropped one on the counter. The Mexican reached out, snatched it up. He pushed the whiskey container forward. "The jug, Senor," he murmured, she is yours." But his eyes did not leave Wate's closed hand.

Another gold piece dropped to the rough counter. Another, and another. The Mexican's eyes lit up, but he stood motionless. Then, he shrugged expressively. "There are no women here, Senor. That is—almost no women. Maria in the kitchen, she is fat. Americans do not like too fat women, no?"

"But there was a woman here, maybe? Slim, brown hair, and so tall?" Wate raised a palm and held it out flat to signify height.

Instantly, the Mexican changed. His look became one of savagery, and his right arm moved with blurring speed. The knife was in his loose sleeve. It came out in a flash of silver together with the Mexican's high scream: "Feelthy gringo! You slap Antonio, you die!"

The knife slipped across Wate's neck, a shade too far to the left, and there was a line of crimson along his throat. He lowered his hand as the Mexican backed away abashed at his own poor aim.

Wate laid the rest of his gold coins on the counter. There was a look of triumph in his eyes as he rounded the counter and stood over the crouched and now terrified Mexican.

"Rise up, greaser," Wate ordered softly.

The Mexican came erect, pressing himself hard against the wall as he cringed from the expected blow.

"It wasn't the slap, was it?" Wate said. "There was another woman—a brown-haired woman so high. She came with a man as big as a young horse, and that man was maybe your friend?"

The Mexican said nothing.

"He gave you gold to make a tight mouth?"

The Mexican's eyes went swiftly to the right and the left as though seeking means of escape. Wate hit him squarely in the mouth with a force that cracked his head against the adobe wall and left a dent. "Enough gold to pay for that?"

The man whined and licked at the blood welling from his lips. He was down again, and Wate bent a knee and pressed it hard against his throat. "Talk, greaser," he said. "Let loose with the

11

lingo, or the Devil will be listening to you in hell."

The Mexican held his throat muscles tight against Wate's knee. His teeth gritted, but his mouth did not open.

"I could take you out in the desert and break your back and leave you for the sun. Did Queen give you enough gold for that?"

The Mexican's throat worked and sounds came out. "I— I will talk, Senor."

"That's better. Get up and have a drink."

The Mexican gulped down a tumbler of whiskey while Wate, lounging with elbows on the counter, dropped another gold piece beside the pile al— ready there.

"You are right, Senor. His name was Queen. A big one. He—"

"Take it easy. Lots of time. Have another drink."

An hour later, the Mexican was sprawled on the floor, holding his whiskey glass high and letting the gold pieces dribble through his fingers.

"...the most beautiful senorita I have ever seen, Senor."

"Only the two of them—Queen and Candy. He must have dropped his gang."

"You are my friend, Senor McCord. Antonio's friend for all days to come. I tell you. I no lie to you."

"Where would Bill Queen go from here?"

The Mexican burped and grinned idiotically. "You and Senor Bill Queen—you are friends?"

"Yes," Wate said patiently. "We are friends. He waits for me in a certain town, but I am stupid and forgot the name."

The Mexican looked around slyly like a child playing a game. Then, he leaned close to Wate breathing rotten whiskey fumes. "Santa Blanca," he whispered throatily. "The Village of the White Saint. Four days to the southeast."

"I will find Queen there?"

Antonio put a finger beside his nose and leered at Wate. "Perhaps. Perhaps not. But on street in Santa Blanca is a place known as the Blue Madonna. A place of singing and dancing, amigo, where the women are beautiful and there are many rooms upstairs..."

The Mexican's voice trailed off and his eyelids drooped. Thirty seconds later, he was snoring with the sound of a dull buzz saw.

Wate left the Mexican lying there against the wall and rode southeast. An elation tingled in his body. He'd found a lead after many weary miles of failure. He traveled steadily at a mile-eating jog. A day and a half out brought him to another adobe. The pattern of it was monotonously familiar. A sun-baked hut. A well, and some sparse green vegetation. Also, a scraped, toothless man sitting by the wall on the shady side of the adobe.

Santa Blanca? The man waved a hand southward with no change whatever in his expression. The days? Two fingers poked into the air.

Wate filled his canteens at the well. When he returned, the man's hand was pushed out, palm upward. Wate dropped a coin into it and went on his way.

He stopped early that night because he came to a small creek and his horse was entitled to a rest. He watered the animal sparingly and staked it out on bare ground for half an hour. Then, he allowed it to drink its fill and wallow luxuriously in the creek.

He fried some bacon for himself and then stretched out in his blanket under the stars. For what seemed hours, he lay wide-eyed, looking up into the darkness. In his mind, there was only one thought— Bill Queen. It had been a long trip and he had cursed the disappointments and the delays, but as things stood now, he'd been lucky. Two months out of Kansas and he was on Queen's trail. He tried not to think of Candy, steeled his mind against it. And finally, he slept.

But only to dream the same old dream.

And now here he was, hugging his knees under a desert sky, with all the horror of the thing fresh again in his mind. He took a deep breath which was really a sob and stretched out wearily on the hard ground. Then came sudden realization.

Something besides the dream had awakened him this time. Hardly registering in his mind, there had been faint, faraway sounds. The sounds were louder now; the crack-crack- crack of irregular gunfire.

Wate got to his feet, reaching unconsciously for his gun belt and buckling it about his hips. Louder came the gun fire and, in the dim light of false dawn, Wate saw the light, can- vas-covered wagon come hurtling to- ward the creek not fifty yards down. The driver of the wagon was not visible, but Wate could see that the two maddened horses were completely beyond control.

Three figures were in pursuit and were gaining steadily. One rider came close to the rear of the wagon and rose in his stirrups with a yell, preparatory to boarding the vehicle. Wate pulled his rifle from the saddle boot at his feet. His gun roared as a streak of red flame shot from the rear of the wagon.

The raider gave forth a single, high- pitched scream as the charge of the heavy gun caught him dead center in the chest and neck. As he fell from his horse, Wate could see the spouting crimson even in the dim light. The man lay where he fell with half his chest torn away.

But the wagon was rushing toward chest with both, knees. The creek loomed close, and there was no chance of pulling the horses to a stop. The front wheels dropped over a sharp, two-foot embankment as the horses, skidding into the creek-bed, trumpeted in terror and went down.

The wagon tongue snapped and buried its short, jagged end into the belly of one of the animals. The wagon itself came on-end over end-with the sound of breaking timbers and ripping canvas.

The two remaining pursuers pulled up momentarily, the sudden disaster taking them by surprise. Wate McCord dropped to one knee and lifted his Remington to his shoulder. The gun barked, and the hat of the near raider flew into the air. The second rider, instantly spotting Wate McCord, swerved low in the saddle and came straight in without a break in stride. Wate's finger pressed the trigger again.

Nothing happened. The rifle had jammed.

Then, the thunder of hooves was close. A giant figure loomed above Wate and hurled itself straight down upon him. Wate stiffened himself against the weight that smashed him to the ground.

Wrenching, turning, seeking leverage, he opened his eyes. Then, for a moment, he lay motionless, stunned by sheer surprise.

He was looking up into the dark, bestial face of Bill Queen.

A roar of rage welled up in McCord's throat. With a sudden, superhuman effort, he came up from the ground, hurling Queen's two-hundred and fifty pounds through the air. Without thought, he followed the path of Queen's body; followed it with a long, clean dive through space, to land squarely upon the big man's chest with both knees. His hands found the thick throat, and the sheer exultation of the moment gave him the strength of five men.

His fingers dug in, found Queen's wind and cut it off. The giant outlaw had been knocked off balance by the fury of McCord's attack. He lay stunned, but only for brief seconds.

In sudden desperation, his arms went around McCord's body, holding him close, and his head came up in a murderous, battering-ram thrust to smash into McCord's face. The force of contact broke McCord's nose and his grip on Queen's throat. McCord flung his head back as the splashing blood filled his eyes and flowed back into his throat, choking him.

Queen slid from under, and both men staggered to their feet at the same time.

McCord, getting set a split second before his giant adversary, shot a straight right in under his heart. Every ounce of McCord's strength went into that blow. It had to stop Queen at least momentarily, or McCord was through. This because the blood, spouting from his nose and from a long cut on his forehead, was hampering McCord, filling his eyes and blinding him, making him an easy mark for the murdering raider.

The blow did stop Queen. His mouth opened and his face mirrored the agony of the fist deep under his heart. He sank to his knees, clawing at the air, and McCord's feeling of hot triumph was complete. Fate had been good to him; had delivered his enemy into his hands.

Then, there was nothing. An explosion on the back of his skull, bright crimson flashing before his eyes. As he went forward, he knew the taste of blood-soaked mud as his mouth hit the ground.

Oblivion.

It was broad daylight when Wate came to. He rolled over, came to a sitting position, and looked blearily about him. No living thing was in sight. The wagon was still there, half in and half out of the now-muddied creek. A quick glance told McCord that both of the horses were dead. One had died from the stabbing wagon tongue and the other had evidently drowned.

A moaning sound came from the wagon. Obviously, someone inside it was still alive. McCord swayed to his feet. He walked to the scene of the wagon wreck, stepped down the embankment, and pulled back the torn canvas that covered the smashed vehicle.

A man lay among the wreckage at the extreme rear end of the buckled wagon. The man raised a bloody head. His mouth worked, but only garbled, throaty sounds came out. The man's first instinct was to fight. He swung one arm in a feeble motion as McCord reached for him.

"It's all right, partner," McCord said. "Take it easy. I was camping here by the creek, and you almost ran me over."

Sudden hope, then relief, appeared in the man's eyes. He was not old, probably in his late twenties, but thin and undernourished to the point of emaciation. Something seemed wrong with his speech. His large, eloquent eyes tried to convey a message to McCord as the latter carried him away from the wagon up to firm ground.

McCord laid him down gently and began examining him for injuries. But the man struggled to a sitting position and waved a desperate hand toward the wagon.

"Somebody else in there?" McCord asked, whereupon the man nodded eagerly and sought to push McCord in that direction. McCord got silently to his feet and returned to the wagon. He opened the back flap and crawled inside.

The wagon had buckled sharply across the middle, and McCord could see why it had not been utterly demolished. An iron strap of fair thickness had been screwed to the bed underneath from fore to aft. This kept the bed itself from splintering aft. This kept the bed itself from splintering.

Instinctvely, she moved an arm to cover her nudity.

He climbed up over the ridge where the strap was bent, and peered into the shambles up front. He saw a mass of tumbled, yellow hair—frosty yellow, like goldenrod on a cold morning—streaked with blood; an almost naked young breast rising and falling, and two slim brown legs, One of her legs was spread-eagled out in an awkward position; a dangerous looking position. From appearances, the leg could have been broken.

17

At that moment, as though conscious of McCord's eyes upon her, the girl turned her head and opened her own eyes. Instinctively, she moved an arm to cover her nudity. Her expression showed only helplessness and despair.

"You've—you've got us," she said, as tears welled up and made clean little rivers on her begrimed face. "What are you going to do with us?"

McCord could not refrain from thinking what Bill Queen would have done under similar circumstances, but the thought dwelt only fleetingly. He was wondering about injuries. Here, far out in the heart of an outlaw land, was no place to care for casualties.

"It's all right, miss," McCord said. "Just as I told the man who's with you—I was camping here and had a ringside seat for the show. You're safe now. I'll help you out and see how bad you're hurt. But first, how about that leg? Is it broken?"

McCord saw gratitude and relief for the second time in a few minutes. "I don't know. I can't move it. It's stuck."

"Let me help you." Gently, Wate took the girl's leg in his hands, at the ankle and just above the knee. "Let me know if I hurt you. Yell quick. If it's broken, we've got to be awfully careful."

Very slowly, he lifted the leg. The girl bit her lip, but said nothing. After he had raised it a few inches to clear the wreckage jammed against it, he stopped and looked at her with concern. "Hurt?"

She shook her head. "I guess it isn't broken. That feels good. Much better."

Wate breathed a sigh of relief. "Put an arm over my shoulder. I'll get you out of here."

The girl reddened now, as though becoming suddenly conscious of her condition. Her eyes pleaded, and then she gave McCord a slight, uncertain smile. "I know this isn't a time to be prudish," she said, "but if I could just have something—a blanket."

McCord reddened himself. "Of course." He turned away and dug around until he found a sizable piece of brown burlap. As the girl sat up, he put it around her smooth brown shoulders. "This will do for the time being. Hold onto me now, and we'll get you out of here."

As he lifted her from the wagon, the girl looked up front and saw the still bodies of the horses. "They're dead?"

"That's right. And you're lucky you aren't dead, too."

He carried the girl up the embankment and laid her down be side the man. For a moment, she lay back with an arm over her eyes. Then, she sat up clutching burlap to her. "I'm all right," she said. "We owe you a great deal for your help." Then, she turned to the silent man. "Are you badly hurt, Neal?"

The man she called Neal shook his head emphatically and made motions indicating the same question.

"No. I guess I'm all right. We were very fortunate. I twisted my ankle and my side hurts a little, but it's just wrenched."

She now turned her attention to McCord. "I'm Patricia Morley," she said. "Neal and I were on the way to a town called Santa Blanca. We'd passed two way-stations and...well, it's a rather long story." She smiled up at him wearily, and put a hand to her aching side.

"My name is McCord," he said. "Wate McCord. You can tell me about it later. Just now, you've got to get some rest. You're fagged out."

""Do you think we're safe? Will they come back?"

"I don't think so." McCord's eyes narrowed at a sudden thought. "You say you passed two way-stations? Just a minute." He turned and strode rapidly off across the desert.

The dead raider. Wate had forgotten him in the rush of subsequent events. Now, pressed on by a strong hunch, he approached the inert and mangled body. He knelt down and turned it over. A moment later, he straightened up with a certain air of satisfaction and stood looking down into the dead face of Antonio—he of the swiftly thrown knife and the voluble, drunken babbling.

This put a new slant to the picture. Somehow, after he'd left the adobe, more than two days rearward, the Mexican had teamed up with Bill Queen for a lawless pursuit of the slight man and the

19

beautiful yellow–haired Patricia Morley. How come? There was little use pondering on it until he had the couple's story. But there was something else—another question for which they would not have the answer. This question loomed large in McCord's mind. Why had Queen left him alive? Obviously, the third raider was responsible for the blow which had felled McCord and sent him into oblivion. But it was an oblivion from which he should never have returned. Why hadn't Queen put a slug into his head and left him to rot away in the desert?

McCord gave this a lot of thought as he went to round up the dead Antonio's horse. The animal was a hundred yards out in the desert, its reins hanging. Evidently having been taught to stand for a ground tie, it traveled by the process of continually circling the fallen reins and moving a little farther away each time it turned.

The horse was skittish, rolling its eyes until the whites«showed large, but it suffered McCord to come close and take the reins. He led the horse back to his camp, thinking the while that it made two mounts for three people. He unsaddled the horse and tethered it near his own.

When he returned, he noted that Patricia Morley had disappeared. Neal answered his unspoken question by nodding in the direction of a sheltered section of the creek. Obviously, the girl had sought privacy to augment her clothing and make herself presentable.

After Patricia had been gone over an hour, McCord frowned and went to the creek. He walked upstream until he came upon the girl stretched on the bank sound asleep. She'd patched up her dress with strips of burlap and had bathed in the stream.

But fatigue had overtaken her in the process. She looked like a tired child, her golden hair spilling out on the grass.

McCord smiled briefly and turned away. He let her sleep for three hours. While she slept, he debated his best course of action. The finding of Antonio engaged in a raid was, when analyzed, no great surprise. Regardless of this, Wate decided he had no reason to doubt the Mexican's information regarding Queen's headquarters. He'd gotten Antonio drunk and had paid him well, and he had a feeling the man had told the truth. Possibly he'd even forgotten the telling when he sobered up.

Besides, Patricia Morley and her strange companion were headed for Santa Blanca, and Wate felt he could hardly desert them now.

So the Village of the White Saint was still his destination, but, because he was in a hurry to be on his way, he had no chance to question the girl until they were on the move shortly after noon. Patricia rode in Wate's saddle with Wate mounted behind her. Neal brought up the rear.

"'What's wrong with him?" Wate asked. "How did he lose his voice?"

Wate felt a shudder ripple through the slim young body so close to his own.

"Not his voice. His...tongue."

"How did it happen?"

"During the war—back in Georgia—on our plantation. It's—are you sure you want to hear it?"

"If you want to tell me."

"Our plantation was burned toward the end of the war, and my mother and I and a few of the men unfit for service were the only ones left there. We struggled along as best we could, and finally mother died."

"I'm sorry."

"Thank you, but it was probably for the best. She lived for quite a while with a broken heart. Anyhow, a band of Northern soldiers stormed through one day—at least, they wore Northern uniforms. Neal saw them coming and didn't like the look of them. He hid me in a root cellar, and I stayed there all night and far into the next day. When I came out, I found that all the other men had run away—all except Neal. The soldiers were gone, too, and I found Neal lying in the yard, half dead from loss of blood."

The girl hesitated, then went on: "It was awful. His—his tongue had been cut out."

She spoke in a low voice, evidently so Neal, riding behind, wouldn't hear her, and McCord could scarcely catch her words.

21

"While I was nursing him, some of the other men straggled in out of the woods. They told me what had happened. Neal had not run away, so the brutes got their hands on him while some of the others watched helplessly from the woods. They told me the leader of the raiders demanded to know where I was. He said he knew there was a girl on the plantation. Neal wouldn't tell them and they tortured him. Then, before they left, this leader did...that to him."

"I doubt if they were Northern soldiers," McCord said quietly. "Toward the end of the war, all sorts of blacklegs and murderers ranged the south, wearing whatever uniform best suited their need. Many of them were caught and shot by both Northern and Southern troops. But some of them were never captured."

Patricia shrugged her slim shoulders. "I don't know. Except they never came back."

"Georgia is a long ways away," McCord said. "How did you and Neal get out here in the Nations?"

My brother came back from the war heartsick and discouraged. When he found the plantation in a shambles and mother dead, he wanted nothing Georgia had to offer. We packed what we had and started west as soon as we heard the news of President Lincoln's assassination. That, I think, was the worst thing that happened to the south."

"It was a terrible blow to the whole country."

"We stayed in St. Louis for a while, the three of us, but Bob had an urge to move on. He heard from someone about Santa Blanca, this settlement in the Nations. It was a lawless country, he knew, but he felt that opportunity lay in getting there first and sticking it out until law and order came."

"He went on alone then?"

"Yes. Neal had a sick spell and needed care. We didn't dream of leaving him, of course, after what he'd done for me, and then too, Bob felt the Nations was no place for a girl until the situation got better. So I stayed in St. Louis to take care of Neal.

"We didn't hear from Bob for over six months, and I began to worry. Finally, I decided to follow him. Neal was a lot better then, so we started out."

"Good lord! It was an impossible trip! I don't see how you got this far!"

She turned and gave him a fleeting smile over her shoulder. "We wouldn't be this far if it hadn't been for you!"

"But– "

"It wasn't so bad. Really. We traveled several hundred miles with a wagon train heading for California. Then, I hired one of the men as a guide, and the three of us struck out south."

"Did the leaders of the train approve this?"

"No, but there was nothing they could do about it. I guess I should have taken their advice, though, because three nights ago, the guide deserted us and we had to go on alone. We never saw him again, but he was decent enough in one way. He left a map showing us the route to follow, indicating the two way-stations."

McCord listened to the amazing tale of this girl's courage.

"Both of you should be dead ten times over," he said gently. "An angel must have you by the hand."

She laughed, somewhat shyly. "No one would have thought so when those men started chasing us."

"Did you cross them on the trail?"

Patricia turned to glance swiftly back at Neal, who rode with his eyes never resting, always searching the landscape. "No. That was rather peculiar. Something– some feeling– told me not to go close to the last way-station, I don't know why. Anyhow, we camped some distance from it and Neal must have gone to check on it after I went to sleep. Anyhow, something very strange happened."

The girl glanced backward again to make sure that Neal was out of earshot, then went on in a whisper. "I woke up with Neal prodding my shoulder. He was greatly excited and he hurried me into the wagon. He drove a while and then I saw the way-station–the adobe– by the light of the half-moon. There was an oil lamp shining through one of the windows."

"Neal drove you to the adobe?"

"No. To within a few hundred yards of it. Then, he left me sitting there and walked to it, carrying his rifle. Everything was quiet, and then I heard a shot and Neal came streaking back to the wagon.

23

He jumped into the seat and whipped the horses into a gallop. Back at the way-station, I could hear people yelling and firing guns."

"Do you know why Neal drove you so close to the place?"

Patricia shook her head. "I never asked him about it. We started off across the desert in the darkness, and that's when an angel really had us by the hand. We should have smashed up a dozen times. The men followed us. Several times I thought we'd lost them, but they got track of us again and‒ well, you know the rest."

McCord was silent for a time. He was possessed of an uneasy feeling that he was being sidetracked from his original objective. Bill Queen. Such a project, he felt, called for a lone hand. Yet, here he was involved with a girl who did not belong in the Nations, and a tortured, mutilated man whose eyes held great bitterness.

In a way, McCord was grateful for the companionship. It helped to keep his mind occupied, to keep him from dwelling night and day on the horrible picture which obsessed his mind‒Bill Queen lifting the screaming Candy onto his horse and carrying her away; the hot, lustful look in Queen's eyes as he held Candy's lush body against him, gloating over what was to come.

"A day and a half at the most," Wate said, "and you'll be with your brother."

"Do you have anyone in Santa Blanca?" the girl asked. "Relatives? Is that why you're going there?"

"I have someone there‒yes. But not a relative," Wate replied grimly. After that, they rode in silence.

Santa Blanca, a collection of adobes plus a scattered few frames on the main business street, was living proof that no place on earth can be entirely evil. A place as foul as Sodom, as dangerous as Port Said, it was the focal point toward which gravitated every blackleg opportunist, every murderer, robber and renegade in the vast unpoliced area known as the Nations.

Yet, it was not entirely evil, because even the damned need to buy and sell, to eat and drink, and to make traffic with the comparatively honest. And wherever there is an out‒ let for their wares, the merchant, the hotel keeper and the restaurateur will set up a business. They were, of course, the hardiest of the breed; those willing to take their chances; men who carried guns and were willing to use them if need be.

And there was even a burlesque of law in the Village of the White Saint − a blustering swashbuckler named Calloway who established his office, hung out a sign reading JUSTICE OF THE PEACE, and went into business without permission from anyone.

Wate McCord was surprised to see the sign. He paused while passing the place and wondered about it, wondered by what authority the Justice functioned. Then, he went on down the main street of Santa Blanca and selected the largest saloon in sight. A paunchy barkeep pushed a bottle toward Wate, took his gold piece and dropped it into a drawer. No saloon in Santa Blanca made change. A man laid down his money and drank until it was gone.

"Nice town you've got here," Wate said. I'm new. Just came in." He dropped another gold piece. The barkeep eyed it with no change of expression and remained silent.

"Looking for a friend of mine. Fellow named−"

"I don't know very many people around here. I just hand out the drinks."

Wate dropped another coin, then frowned. "Let's stop being coy. How much will it cost me to locate a man named Bob Morley. He's probably in business somewhere on the street."

The barkeep relaxed. He picked up the gold and leaned fat forearms on the bar. "That won't cost you much at all, mister. The name's familiar. You go up to the north end of the street and turn to the left. Ride a quarter of a mile and look around. You'll find him."

"What kind of business is he in?"

The barkeep grinned. "He ain't in no business at all. He's in the cemetery."

Wate set his glass down very slowly, stared at it for a moment, then raised his eyes to the barkeep. "How did it happen?"

"Gun fracas in the street. He was murdered, I guess you'd call it, but the other man paid the penalty." The barkeep chuckled. "Paid for his crime, you might say."

"Was he hung?"

"Naw! It was only a killing. He was fined ten dollars and costs by Justice Calloway. The costs was twenty-five dollars. Nigh broke the man, it did." The barkeep threw back his head and emitted a toothy laugh.

When he was through, Wate asked, "Where can I find a yellow-belly named Bill Queen?"

The barkeep dropped his levity like an old overcoat. His face went blank, his eyes flat and impersonal. "Never heard the name, mister. You want another drink?"

McCord turned from the bar and went out into the street. He retraced his steps until he was standing under the sign reading: JUSTICE OF THE PEACE. He went inside.

A crude railing separated him from a large desk at which a mustached, elderly man sat with his hat tipped forward over his eyes. The man was dozing.

"Your name Calloway?" Wate asked.

A hand came up to push the hat back. A pair of ice-blue eyes surveyed Wate from head to toe. There was insolence in the eyes and the face. The features were built to mirror insolence.

"*Justice of thee Peace* Calloway, son. Don't ever forget that handle. It's important."

"I'm looking for information about a man named Robert Morley. Maybe you can help me out?"

Calloway's jaws were moving rhythmically now. He pursed his lips and shot a stream of tobacco juice into a clay pot standing in a corner. His eyes squinted thoughtfully. "Morley. . . Morley. . . He ever appear before me?"

"Not that I know of. But I understand his murderer did."

"Oh, sure. I recollect now. About three months ago it was. Seems to me he took affront at a remark some hombre made in the street and pulled a gun on him. The hombre was a mite faster than Morley and killed him. The jasper claimed self defense, but I gave Morley the benefit of the doubt 'cause he was dead and couldn't testify in his own behalf. I fined the jasper that killed him, thus putting the onus of murder on the said hombre."

"By what authority do you function?" Wate asked.

Calloway scowled and got slowly to his feet. "Now, listen here, young fellow. If you're looking for trouble—"

"I merely asked the question. Why should that lead to trouble?"

"I function by my own authority. Want to make an issue out of it?"

"I didn't say that."

Calloway sat down, still scowling. "Well, you better not. Wouldn't be healthy."

"Did Morley leave anything? Any estate?"

"Nothing to speak of," Calloway returned levelly. "A pocket knife and a .45 Colt. They're laying around here somewhere, I guess. I'll look them up if you insist."

"I guess it doesn't matter. I wouldn't want to put you to any trouble."

The sarcasm apparently went over Calloway's head. "And I guess the mud house he put up out in the yucca could be called his. Nobody else wants it."

"A house?"

"Uh-huh. About four miles due west of town. The jasper had some cock-eyed idea of starting a herd. Plumb foolishness, of course. He drilled a well and damned if he didn't hit water, but it'll dry up, if it hasn't already. No water lasts out here."

"Would there be any objection to his sister taking it over?"

Calloway's brows went up.

"Did the jasper have a sister?"

"That's right. I rode into town with her."

The mustachioed rascal considered this. "No...don't see why anybody'd object. But there's nothing to take over. Who in tarnation'd want a mud house out in the desert?"

"What about his herd?"

"He'd just gotten started," Calloway returned. "Had himself a few bone-yard longhorns as I recollect."

"What happened to them?"

"Well, now—that I don't know. With nobody to tend them, I guess they must have wandered away." There was a moment of dead silence. "Yes, sir, that's probably just what happened. Them critters wandered away."

McCord's good sense told him it was foolish, under the circumstances, to antagonize this scaly old reprobate.

He gritted his teeth and walked swiftly out of the office. This because he was close to reaching across the railing and taking the man by the throat.

Once outside in the street, his anger cooled, was washed away by the starker and more immediate job at hand. He had to tell Patricia Morley, waiting in a room at the town's only hotel, that her brother was dead. He shrank from this duty, but his feet led him, nonetheless, along the boardwalk until he stood in front of the hotel. He entered and slowly mounted the steps to the second floor. After holding his knuckles poised for a full half-minute, he rapped on the panel.

There was the sound of quick running feet beyond the door. Then, Patricia Morley was framed in the opening and it struck McCord forcibly for the first time—this girl was beautiful. There was more than mere beauty, however. He was looking at the clear freshness of youth, the indefinable something that makes every girl beautiful in the eyes of a man. That mystical quality which, once despoiled, never returns.

It went through McCord's mind like a knife thrust that Candy Thompson had had that quality but a few short weeks before. Now, it would be gone from her forever.

He entered the room and closed the door behind him. Patricia, her eyes questioning, stood before him in silence. He put his hands on her shoulders and forced her gently backwards until the backs of her thighs touched the bed.

"Sit down," he said quietly.

She sat with hands folded looking up at him, and the complete trust in her expression hit him like a tangible pain.

"Did you find Bob? Is he coming?"

McCord fumbled for words and could find none. Then, he

decided there was no se trying to soften a blow that could not be softened.

"Your brother is dead," he told her. The color washed from her face.

Her lips opened, closed again. Her hand came up to press against his chest as though fending him off. He took the hand in his and held it tight.

"He was shot down in the street. Killed in a gun fight. I didn't get any of the details. In a place like this—in times like these—details don't matter much. We just have to accept the facts."

He had made no attempt to forecast her reactions. He'd kept his mind blank on this point. She sat perfectly still for a time, then slowly withdrew her hand from his. Seated on the bed, she was staring straight at his belt buckle. He stepped aside, but her eyes remained set. They were now looking at the cracked water pitcher on the washstand.

He said, "I'm sorry. I'm very sorry. I wish there was something I could do."

"Please go away. Please leave me alone for—for an hour. I want to be alone now. I hope I don't sound ungrateful. I—I just want to be by myself."

"I understand." He moved toward the door, then turned. "Do you know where Neal is? I'll tell him."

She shook her head. "No. Leave that to me. Besides, I don't know where he is. He's around the town somewhere."

McCord closed the door and went downstairs into the lobby of the hotel. At the foot of the stairs he stopped short, frowning. With the air of a man in deep thought, he reached into his shirt pocket, brought out papers and a bag of tobacco, and began rolling a cigarette.

His frown deepened. Just what kind of a business was he becoming involved in? What did it matter to him whether Bob Morley had been killed or not? It wasn' t his responsibility. Neither was he obligated to worry about the yellow-haired girl upstairs who didn't have sense enough to stay where her brother had left her.

He, McCord, had come to Santa Blanca for one reason alone—to do a single job—and he had no intention of being sidetracked. He'd done the humane thing regarding Patricia Morley. He'd picked her up in the desert and had brought her to her destination. So far as he was concerned, that ended it. He had some business of his own, and that business was named Bill Queen. He wanted only to find the man, and find him quick. With this thought in mind, he lit his cigarette and walked out on the porch of the hotel.

He raised his eyes and saw Bill Queen, riding a skittish buckskin, riding directly past him up the street.

McCord let out a single exultant yell—a sound not unlike that of an Apache war whoop. Then: "You! Queen!" in a voice heard far up and down the street.

Bill Queen's head came around as though jerked by a string. In the same motion, his hand went for his gun. But he was far too slow to escape the slugs from McCord's .45 Colt. It was something entirely different that saved him from coughing out his life in the middle of the street.

As McCord's shoulders hunched and his hand closed over the butt of his gun, a dead weight hit him solidly from behind—from the doorway of the hotel through which he'd just stepped. Completely losing his balance, he hurtled forward, pushed out one leg to save himself, and sprawled full length on the porch behind the waist- high horizontal planking, which separated the porch from the boardwalk beyond.

As he went down, he heard the sudden flurry of hoof-beats in the street —hoofbeats diminishing—as Bill Queen raked his buckskin on up the street, then flung himself from the saddle and disappeared between two buildings.

In a high rage, McCord rolled over and came to his knees. Then, he froze in consternation as he spotted his attacker.

It was Neal.

McCord came slowly erect, staring in sheer surprise at the thin little man. Neal was lying full length on the porch, looking up at McCord with fear in his face. While McCord stood open-mouthed, struggling for words, Neal went into a desperate pantomime, which would have been funny under other circumstances.

He came to his knees and pointed at the doorsill, then at his own foot. Jumping to his feet, he scurried back into the hotel, only to turn around and emerge again, catching his toe on the sill and falling headlong. Then he lay still, his eyes begging McCord to understand.

What he intended to show was obvious. He'd come through the door way behind McCord, had tripped, fallen against the latter, and had knocked him flat.

With a curse, McCord was off the porch and running up the street. He plunged headlong into the narrow areaway between the two buildings where Queen had disappeared. He ran the length of it, leaped into the open at the rear end and stood crouched, ready for action.

But there was no one to act against. A Mexican who had been squatting, asleep, beside the wall of the building, opened his eyes and regarded McCord with wonder. Then, as McCord retreated into the areaway as he had come, the Mexican shrugged, closed his eyes and returned to siesta.

McCord walked on up the street and turned into the door of the first saloon he came to. He downed two quick drinks and stood there with his elbows on the bar, scowling into a cracked mirror.

His thoughts were centered on the occurrence of the preceding few minutes. What was going on anyhow? Were the fates playing with him? Were the laws of chance in conspiracy to see that he put no slugs into Bill Queen? Two opportunities had been afforded him. In the first, he'd been fortunate to come away with his own life. In the second, he'd been knocked flat by a clumsy mute in the very act of sending his bullets home.

Then, the suspicion hit him squarely: Had Neal stumbled by chance, or by design? If by chance, the coincidence was staggering. He'd made the only possible move that could have saved Queen's life.

McCord's mind went back to that other incident Patricia had told him about: Neal's mysterious action at the way-station. What shots had been fired by whom?

Neal, McCord told himself, was somehow allied with Bill Queen; was seeking to protect him. Projecting this supposition starkly, McCord now sought to analyze it.

How could such a thing be possible? Where had Neal originally made contact with the thieving cutthroat? And, if he were truly in league with the man, why had he fled across the desert that night? And why had Queen and his men been in such murderous pursuit?

Neal's treachery seemed impossible, yet it was the only logical answer to subsequent happenings.

Unless Neal's fall had been truly an accident.

Still pondering the problem, Wate walked out into the street. Pie stood on the walk and his thoughts switched to his more pressing problem—Bill Queen. He looked up and down the long street, wondering if a house-to-house search would be feasible. He decided against it. Queen knew the town, McCord did not. Queen certainly had friends in this brigand's stronghold. McCord was all alone.

Wate shrugged and walked toward the hotel. A few moments later, he was knocking on Patricia Morley's door. When the door opened, he found himself looking into the dark, inquiring eyes of Neal. The man stepped back and McCord walked into the room.

Patricia sat huddled in the only chair provided. Her beautiful oval face was pale, her eyes were red from weeping, but she was now composed.

It's good that she could cry, McCord thought. Then he said, "I was told of a place your brother built about four miles out of town. It was his home, no doubt. I'll take you there if you wish."

There was only the slightest tremor in her voice. "I'd like it very much. You've been good to us, very good."

She arose from the chair and McCord turned toward the door. Half way into the hall, he stopped and looked back. His gaze, frankly hostile, was on Neal. "Is he going too?"

"I—I think he'd like to," Patricia said. "If it wouldn't be too much trouble."

"No trouble at all," McCord said gruffly. "I'll get the horses and see about renting a third one."

They rode out into the desert from the Village of the White Saint, McCord and Patricia Morley side by side, and Neal bringing up the rear as usual.

"What is he to you?" Wate asked, indicating Neal with a backward jerk of his head. "What did he do in Georgia?"

"He's a very distant relative by marriage—just how distant I don't know. His people were very poor. They had nothing at all, and Neal came to stay with us."

"Is he—do you trust him?"

Quick surprise came into Patricia's face. "Trust him? Why, of course. I told you what he did for me. I'd trust him with my life. Why do you ask?"

McCord frowned. "Oh, I don't know. Maybe it's this town. This country. Living in this hell hole, a man might be doubtful about his best friend."

Ahead of them, two adobe buildings and a crude pole corral shimmered in the high sun. The buildings stood on comparatively high ground —a sort of low mesa—and were apparently deserted. They looked shabby, almost cringing, against the incredible vastness of the mesquite and cactus dotted plain.

McCord surveyed them with slitted eyes. "I wonder how your brother expected to raise cattle in this God-forsaken place?"

Patricia's head came up proudly. "I don't know," she said. "But then, you didn't know Bob. He would have accomplished it, whatever the odds."

"I'm sure he would," McCord said, and swung down from his horse in front of the larger of the two buildings.

Patricia came quickly to his side. "Would you—would you mind," she asked shyly, "if I went in first— alone? Maybe it's silly, but—"

"I understand. Neal and I will look the shed over."

McCord turned and strode toward the small building a couple of hundred yards away. When he reached it, he turned and looked back. Patricia had vanished, and Neal had not accompanied McCord. The thin little man stood by his horse's head stood motionless, his eyes staring off into pace while he rubbed the animal's nose. McCord went into the shed and stood peering around in the comparative darkness.

But his mind was elsewhere. On Bill Queen. Queen certainly knew, by this time, that McCord wasn't in Santa Blanca by chance. The big raider couldn't help knowing his life was McCord's grim objective. Then what was he doing, what plans was he making to protect himself?

Again McCord's mind wandered to the question, which continued to plague him. Why had Queen spared his life there at the creek? And, for that matter, why had he spared Neal's life and left Patricia Morley unmolested? As luscious a creature as Patricia should certainly have been a natural target for the black-hearted Queen's lust, just as–McCord's face darkened and his eyes grew bitter– just as the body of Candy Thompson must have served to satiate that same lust.

McCord scowled. There was an infuriating frustration in this whole affair–a chain of unanswered questions that nagged at McCord's mind and gave hint of ominous things to come. McCord's instinct told him that all was not as it seemed–that a great volcano of human passions was close to the blowing point, and that the volcano was soon to explode about his ears.

He estimated a half hour had passed, and turned his steps toward the larger building. Neal, he noted, had not moved from his position. He still stood by his mount's head, stroking the animal's velvet nose and staring off into space.

McCord walked past him and approached the open door of the adobe. He stepped inside. The room was crudely, yet neatly furnished. All the pieces were obviously hand made by someone with not too much skill in that sort of thing. McCord went on through into the second room. He stopped in the doorway, came to an abrupt halt to keep from running into Patricia Morley.

The girl was standing just inside, oblivious of everything, even McCord's approaching footsteps. Suddenly sensing his presence, she came out of her solitary reverie and whirled in alarm. The movement threw her squarely into McCord's arms.

She uttered a small, choked cry and McCord could feel the pressure of her breasts against his chest. The quick gust of her breathing was full in his face with her lips just an inch beyond.

They stood frozen in this posture for a limitless moment, her eyes wide and staring directly into his. A look of wonder, of sudden awakening was in her face.

And, far back in McCord's mind was an understanding of the moment. His senses stirred; they could scarcely have done otherwise with Patricia Morley so close. Her beautiful body pressing in would have stirred a man of stone.

But McCord's thought was: She's almost as beautiful and warm and desirable as Candy.

Another instant and her arms would have been tight around his neck, her lips hard against his own. But during that moment, McCord was again seeing the look, the terror on Candy's face as she fought Queen that night—the night of her defilement.

McCord, his throat tight, pushed Patricia gently backward. "I'm sorry," he said. "I didn't mean to startle you."

She drew away and sought to compose herself. "It's all right," she said, lowering her eyes. "I guess I was lost in my own thoughts

"I'm going to try and find out who killed your brother," McCord said. "We'll even up the score."

Then he bit his lip, turned away and frowned. Why had he said that? Why should he risk his life to get the killer of a man he didn't even know? What business was it of his?

McCord, he thought sourly, you're quite a fellow. Got any grievances, anybody? Just bring them to Wate McCord. He's in the business of squaring accounts. The line forms to the right, and don't crowd.

Patricia's voice broke into his thoughts: "No," she said quietly. "Violence isn't the answer to violence. Killing doesn't avenge killing. It just makes more sorrow, more bloodshed, more misery. I learned that back in Georgia."

While he gave scant thought to her philosophy, McCord welcomed her words; welcomed the release from his rash, stupid promise. "Don't you think we'd better be getting back now?"

She nodded. "I'm glad I came, but I don't ever want to come again. This is all part of the past now. Bob took it from the desert and the desert can take it back. I want to remember him the way he was when he waved good bye at St. Louis."

"I understand," Wate said.

As they dismounted in front of the hotel, he said, "You'd better go up and rest now. Stay in your room and get a good night's sleep. Tomorrow we'll talk things over. You can tell me what your plans are."

She smiled at him. "I am tired," she said.

McCord turned the horses over to Neal and moved off up the board sidewalk. He had no idea where he was going. He only knew that he was completely discouraged with his progress so far, and thus in a low and somewhat truculent mood.

Then he stopped suddenly, so suddenly, that the man walking behind bumped him sharply, and cursed as he went around and on by.

The Blue Madonna!

What had he been using for brains? McCord wondered. He'd given Antonio a sizable amount of gold and had filled him with whisky to elicit information. Then, in the rush of events, he'd allowed an important part of what he'd learned to slip his mind.

Instantly, the whole world brightened for McCord. The Blue Madonna. It was an integral part of this puzzle he was involved in. Possibly the end of his trail. McCord straightened his shoulder and moved on down the street. His eyes now alert, watching every saloon he passed for that name.

The Blue Madonna. He found it on a side street just off the main avenue of traffic. A small, unpretentious sign hung over the doorway, but the building—as buildings went in Santa Blanca—was a large one. It was two stories high, but McCord found upon looking it over that the second floor extended only halfway back. The rear half of the building was only one floor under a low, flat roof.

McCord had walked on past the door. Now, he turned and retraced his steps. Glancing up and down the quiet side street, he hitched his gun belt into a snug fit around his hips, and opened the door.

The sound of a well-played guitar and a pair of rhythm gourds hit his ears as McCord's eyes knifed around the large room, locating the various exits and getting the general layout. There was a bar at the far end, and a dozen or so tables were strung out along the near wall. A stage occupied most of the other side, with stair— ways leading upward at both ends of the stage.

Four musicians sat in front of the raised stage, two of them motionless, the other two languidly furnishing the music by which a slim, flame-like girl danced. She wasn't a very good dancer, and sought to cover her deficiency by a great deal of heel clicking. But her smile was attractive, and she seemed sincerely eager to please. A few customers sat at the tables, and there was noisy applause when the girl finished her number and whirled off the stage in a flash of crimson skirts.

McCord dropped into a chair. He chose a table in a dark corner. So secluded was the spot that the waiter did not locate him for some five minutes. During that time, McCord sat tense, his eyes continually on the move. He had a fleeting hope that fate, having frustrated him so far, would favor him to the extent of bringing Bill Queen into view.

But the big man failed to appear. There were several characters who matched him in arrogant and sinister appearance, but no Bill Queen.

Then, the waiter was at McCord's elbow, his voice soft, insistent: "Refreshment, *Senor?*"

"Whisky," McCord said.

The waiter drifted toward the bar and McCord reached down, unconsciously, and loosened his gun in its leather. A few restless eyes passed his way, came back to inspect him, but always traveled on. Evidently, no one recognized him as the man who'd tried to throw down on Bill Queen a few hours before. For this good for— tune, McCord was thankful, but he remained wary nonetheless.

He had previously noticed that the wall behind him was pierced at intervals by arched passages leading into some kind of a hallway along that side of the building. With this in mind, he had seated himself so he could cover both these openings and the main area of the room, also.

Thus, when he turned his head at the sound of footsteps, he was able to see quite clearly the girl who stepped through one of the archways.

It was Candy Thompson.

McCord tensed. Without thinking, he came half out of his chair and was poised there, gripping the edge of the table with hard hands. His mouth opened. Her name formed on his lips. But it was never uttered.

At the same instant, Candy's eyes had found him there at the table, and it was her expression that held him frozen. He had never given any thought to what he would see in Candy's face when they met. He would have possibly expected a surge of happiness; maybe the sheer gratitude he'd found in Patricia Morley back in the wagon on the creek.

But Candy's reaction was one of pure, unadulterated fear.

The look of terror froze McCord into his crouched position, and at that moment, as though carefully staged, there was a high, thin scream, that of a woman in pain. The scream was muffled, coming from somewhere above, somewhere beyond thick walls.

At the sound of it, a few customers grinned and leered at each other. There was coarse laughter and knowing winks. Then, music welled up to cover the scream. But it wasn't necessary now. There was only silence from above.

McCord had been entirely oblivious of all this. He had had eyes and thoughts only for Candy. At that moment, Queen could have walked up and killed him with impunity. McCord was on his feet now, but again he froze as Candy motioned desperately, a sweep of her hand as though pushing him backward into his chair.

Then her eyes went swiftly around the room. Apparently, no one was paying any attention. She moved close to McCord. Her whisper was urgent, pleading: "Go! Please, Wate. Please! Leave this instant and never come back! Do it for me!"

Only for a moment did she remain close to him. Immediately, she drew away and moved off across the room between the tables and toward the stairway at the left of the stage. She went swiftly up the stairs and vanished without looking back.

McCord's mind was working again. He had to talk to Candy. He had to find out what was behind her strange action. She should have come to him and stayed by his side while he fought his way out of this place, if fighting became necessary. Had Queen tortured her, degraded her to the point where her spirit was entirely gone and she could know nothing but pure animal fear?

McCord stood by the table, his, hand on his gun. Up the stairs after her, he thought. Then, as quickly, he rejected this idea. He might reach Candy, but he would have no time to discover what had happened to her, and certainly no opportunity to get her away from the place.

He was not misled by the seemingly placid appearance of his surroundings. If this was Queen's stronghold, as it most certainly was, McCord's life wasn't worth a peso inside these doors. He had been left alone only because he'd been overlooked, because no one knew who he was. He had to reach Candy's side, however, and the only way to do it lay through stealth.

Throwing a gold piece on the table, he made a leisurely exit. He forced this upon himself; walked slowly toward the door with the muscles of his back tightened against a possible bullet, his ears attuned for the sudden crash of gunfire. None came. He closed the door behind him, continued at a casual pace up the walk until he came to the narrow alley beside the building. He ducked inside and found himself in almost complete darkness.

It wasn't too hard to achieve the roof of the one-floor rear section of the building. He found a barrel beside the closed and barred back door; a barrel seemingly put there for the purpose.

The light from two shaded windows helped McCord find his way along the roof. His footsteps were muted by blankets spread on the dried-mud surface. Evidently, the roof was used for siestas. The door to the second floor hallway beyond was closed and barred. But the door did not fit well, and McCord found that it was held by an ordinary wooden slat turning, probably, on a single nail inside. He pushed the blade of his knife through the wide space next to the jamb and found that this was true. The slat turned silently on its pivot. He opened the door slowly, and closed it without a sound.

Two lamps on wall brackets furnished the illumination by which McCord could see a series of doors set opposite each other at intervals along the hall. Working slowly, he tried the first of these. It was locked. He pressed his ear to the panel and could hear nothing.

He passed on to the next.

He turned the knob softly, pushed it open, and a line of yellow lamplight was revealed. There were no sounds from within. He pushed the door wider. A voice, tired, but striving to be cheerful, said, "Don't be bashful, handsome. Come on in. I'm lonesome tonight."

The girl stood beside the bed clad in a blue kirnono. She was smiling, but there was instinctive defiance in her attitude as she stood with her hands on her hips, her head held high, the kimono open to reveal the naked body she had for sale.

McCord closed the door and stood waiting in the hall to see what the girl would do. She did nothing. McCord scowled and moved on up the hall. He almost turned the knob of the next door before he heard the low male voice beyond the panel. He backed carefully away and put his ear to the door opposite.

Stifled sobs came into his ear. He turned the knob and pushed inward. This room was also lighted and there was a bed, but the girl inside was not cheerfully defiant. She lay on the bed with her kimono pulled tight about her. She was crying softly her head buried in her arms. She sensed rather than heard Wate and turned her head. Wate saw a white face and a pair of frightened eyes as he pulled the door shut. It hadn't been necessary for him to see the girl's face. Her hair was jet black. Her name was not Candy.

Wate investigated two more doors. Low voices—those of a man and a woman—came from beyond the first. Wate opened the second. He found a luxuriously furnished living room— no bed here— with Candy standing by the single window looking out into the dark night.

She turned and faced him with no apparent surprise whatever. "Hello, Wate. I've been expecting you. Somehow, I knew you'd find your way up here."

McCord was drinking her in while his heart pounded in his throat. "Candy! Candy—my darling!"

He took a quick step forward, then froze as her hand came up as though to fend him off. There was neither gladness nor welcome in her voice. "No, Wate— no. Don't come any closer. Sit there— on that bench. And don't raise your voice. It would mean your life if they heard you."

Wate sat down, his face a study in wonderment and surprise. "But, Candy— I've come for you! I'm taking you away from here. Do you have a wrap of some kind? We'll go out over the back roof, and then, when you're safely away, I'll come back and—"

She shook her head, a little smile playing sadly on her lips. "No, Wate. You must leave." And the wonder in the man increased. There's pity in her voice, he thought. But not for herself. Pity for me!

It was beyond understanding. Then, he felt what to him was the obvious truth, and his anguish and all his manhood raved and writhed within him: He's broken her. He's raped and beaten and smashed the spirit out of her. She's still walking around and breathing and speaking, but Candy— the Candy I loved—is dead. She's dead.

The girl appeared to divine the trend of his thoughts. "I know what's in your mind," she said, "but it doesn't matter. I'm not the same girl you knew in Kansas. That was a long, long time ago— "

"Only two months, darling." His hands were white as they clutched the edge of the bench.

"A couple of life times ago, Wate. Sometimes, a complete life time can be crowded into a minute— an hour."

"The yellow swine has ruined—"

A slight bitterness came into her smile. "Ruined me? Yes, I suppose so. That's the word the honest, respectable people use in a case like this, isn't it?"

A look of agony came to his face; pure anguish. "My Candy," he said in a harsh whisper, "trapped in a place like this.... "

"I'm not a harlot, if that's what you mean," she said. "No men are sent to my room. In fact, I've known only one man—only one."

The last words were like a hot iron plunged into Wate's pounding heart. His face darkened, and the veins stood out in his throat. He got to his feet in a sort of animal crouch, as though trying to control himself, but not succeeding.

"Where can I find him?" he asked, and suddenly all restraints were gone. Wate had passed the point where he could listen to reason and hold himself in. His voice rose to a yell: "Where can I find the crawling swine? If he's too yellow to fight with guns, we'll use knives or clubs or fists! I'll tear his black heart out and jam it down his throat clear into his stinking yellow belly! Where is he?"

Wate had turned, gun in hand now, and was striding toward the door. Candy, an arm across her throat, was pressed hard against the wall. "No. No, Wate—for God's sake, no! They'll kill you as though they were stamping on a fly. You haven't a chance. Go, while there's still time."

"That's swell," Wate bellowed. "I feel like being stomped on, but God help the man that tries it!"

There had been instant response to his raised voice. The sound of doors opening in the hallway outside, and footsteps running to converge on the door to Candy's room. The door flew open. Crowded in the hallway outside were at least half a dozen men. Wate caught the flash of swarthy Mexican faces, pale gamblers' faces, bearded and whiskered outlaw faces.

The men piled into the room. But not with impunity. There was the tight mirthless grin on McCord's face as he brought his gun up and sent red fire spouting from its muzzle.

The roar of the gun thundered in the small room, covering the scream of the man who stood in wide-eyed surprise as his life and his blood gushed from a hole in his neck; the sick whine from the next in line who doubled over two hot slugs that blasted his belt buckle clear back into his mutilated guts. The man doubled over himself and melted to the floor just in time to open the way for Wate's fourth slug. It blew away the space between the next man's eyes, leaving a great gaping hole. The man's mouth flew open a moment after he died, and the size and shape of both openings were oddly the same. He looked like a man with two mouths as he went headlong on his face.

Wate's two remaining slugs slapped into the paunch of an aproned man, obviously a bartender, and sent him down groveling in agony.

With a sweep of his arm, Wate threw his weapon at the closest head. The head belonged to a thick-lipped desperado who went down as his skull cracked with the sound of a splitting pumpkin.

Wate's advantage lay in the surprise of his attack. The intruders had come expecting to find nothing more serious than a customer possibly disgruntled over the price of an hour of love. Instead, they'd run headlong into a murdering juggernaut—a berserk killer who fought with calm and deadly precision.

Naturally, there was no generalship in the ranks of the intruders. They died like cattle in a slaughtering pen, and when Wate's ammunition was gone, they were in the act of retreating as fast as possible.

As they crowded out through the doorway, eager to get clear of this crazed killer, Wate caught the hindmost squarely on the back of the skull with the unyielding edge of a heavy chair-seat. The man went down with a single squall of pain and lay motionless.

They died like cattle in a slaughtering pen.

Wate seized the hand of the cowering Candy and swept her out into the hall. No one obstructed the passage rearward to the roof, except a naked girl who had stepped from one of the rooms to see what was going on. She ducked back inside quickly as Wate picked Candy up and carried her out onto the roof.

"No, Wate—no! I can't go with you! Leave me here. You can never get away unless you make the break alone."

He didn't seem to hear her. As though she were weightless, he swung her over the roof edge until her feet touched the barrel by the wall. "Jump down," he said, and then he was beside her in the small area backing the building.

But it was nothing more than a trap.

The recuperative powers of the Blue Madonna thugs was astounding. Slaughtered, crushed and cut to ribbons on the second floor, they had been able to rally and get set to smother McCord as he made his exit. They were waiting for him there behind the building. He could as well have dropped off the roof into a rattlesnake pit.

He never knew how many men jumped him there in the darkness. When he became aware of their presence, he pushed Candy back against the doorframe and swung a fist at the closest jaw as he reached for his knife. His fist found a jawbone, but his other arm was locked tight against his side as he sought to slash out with his blade.

Then, they were upon him from all sides. Murderous fists, boots and knees. In such close quarters, they used neither knives nor guns, but they wrought murderous damage just the same. A knee crashed into Wate's groin, doubling him up, throwing him out of defensive position. Then, there followed a couple of minutes of in credible brutality and savageness. Adrift in a sea of agony, Wate heard a voice screaming, imploring, even commanding. Candy's voice: "No! No! Stop it, I tell you. Queen wouldn't want him killed. He was only drunk—looking for a good time!"

Oddly, there was a break in the ranks bearing him down. A pause, as though from surprise. Another voice, low pitched, but tinged with wry amusement: *"Carramba, Senorital* A good time, you tell us. With a half dozen dead in as many moments, one would say this madman has enjoyed himself to the limit. *Madre Dias!* I would hate to meet him in a serious mood."

"Take him to the Justice," Candy was urging feverishly. "Let the Justice sentence and hang him. Would not a hanging be more to your liking?"

Suddenly, McCord became aware of the true temper around him. These men, strangely enough, were not in a vicious mood. In his dazed mind, he sought an answer, and could only decide that there was no brotherhood among outlaws of this type. The dead meant nothing to those still alive. These men, while seeking each other's company, played lone hands and had no feeling for the dead ones. They did not know, of course, who he was. Candy's words had indicated this. He was to them merely a stranger whom they would enjoy seeing at the end of a rope. The hanging, no doubt, would be good fun. Either that, or Candy was the voice of authority in this place. She'd said Queen wouldn't want him dead!

As he was jerked roughly to his feet, McCord found himself again face to face with the unanswered question: Why was Queen loathe to deal out death to his relentless pursuer? It was beyond McCord, and he shook his head groggily as he was forced along through the dark passage toward the street. Somewhere in that areaway, there in the darkness, McCord felt soft hair brushing against his bloody face and heard Candy's whisper: "The Justice will hang you, Wate. He's had six men hung in the last two weeks. I can't protect you from him, so you've got to escape. Make a break for it, Wate! All I got you was a little time."

Then, Candy was gone and McCord was being pushed and dragged up the street. The residents of this town—a town well inured to violence and the sight of blood— stopped to stare at the bloody beaten thing that was Wate McCord. They were used to gory sights, but they'd never seen anything quite like this. McCord stumbled along trying to clear his mind and to draw on his reserve of strength. But a breakaway, under the circumstances, was impossible. He could already feel the hangman's rope tight around his neck.

Justice of the Peace Calloway held court in his office. He sat at his desk while the defendant and the complainants crowded the space beyond the crude railing. He had a gavel with which he pounded the desk and stilled the babbling of the men who'd brought Wate before him.

"Quiet down now, or I'll fine the lot of you for contempt of court. We'll have dignity in here or, by God, I'll know the reason why."

The talking stopped, and Calloway hit the desk again. "This court is now in session. Speak up, somebody–" He pointed his gavel at the ruffian who was clutching Wate's right arm. "–You. State the complaint."

The man grinned happily. "Why sure, Your Honor. This jasper ain't fit to live with decent folks. He comes in and starts shooting up the place for no reason at all. Kills four or five men that had no grudge against him at all. We want to see this hombre hanging by his neck, but the girl–" The man glanced around and seemed surprised that Candy was not present, "–the girl she wants it done legal-like, and we ain't got no objections."

"Kills four or five men in what place?" Calloway demanded, glowering at Wate.

"In the Blue Madonna, Your Honor. He pulled his gun in one of the upstairs rooms."

McCord was certain that he saw an immediate change in Calloway. The scowl remained on the man's face, but it appeared to become less personal, more abstract.

"Bill Queen's place," Calloway said to no one in particular.

But immediately the tenor of the affair changed. Calloway turned his scowl on the crew of vicious complainants. "What was he doing in the room?"

"He was there with one of the girls"

"Did he kill the girl?"

"No. He started yelling and we went in–"

That seemed to cause indignation at the bench. Calloway's frown deepened. "You broke in on him then? Is that it?"

"We sure did. He started blasting– right into us."

47

"Where's the evidence?" Calloway demanded.

The big man on Wate's right asked, "Evidence? What evidence?"

"You said he killed four or five men. You don't expect me to take your word for that. The court's got to see the evidence with its own eyes."

"Then come on over and look at them. They're spread all over the upstairs hall, if they ain't been hauled out yet."

"That's contempt," Calloway roared, banging the, desk. "It's beneath the dignity of the court to be seen in that kind of a place for whatever reason," he said.

"Well, we sure ain't going to lug them over here."

"Then you've got no case. As a matter of fact, I'm inclined to think this man was only defending himself. You probably intended to rob him. Case dismissed."

Consternation held the men tongue-tied. They dropped McCord's arms and stood staring at Calloway. The ringleader muttered, "Well, for—"

"Silence," Calloway bellowed. He banged the gavel. "Clear the court now and leave the prisoner in my charge. I'll investigate further in the morning."

"You'll do some talking to Queen, I'm thinking," the ringleader growled.

"I'll talk to Queen any time. Now, clear the court!"

To McCord, it was miraculous that they did as they were ordered. The last to go was the big man who'd done the talking. As he went out, he had the last word: "I got a hunch you'll swing from a pole yourself, Calloway."

Then, McCord was alone with the Justice of the Peace.

Calloway inspected him critically. "They sure gave you what for, young fellow. Better come in the back room and clean up."

McCord grinned from sheer relief. He did not know by what process he'd escaped death, but he took his new lease on life with relish.

While McCord cleaned himself up in the backroom of

Calloway's "court", the self-styled Justice sat watching Wate's every move.

Conscious of the close scrutiny, Wate said, "Looks to me as though you went out on a limb. I can't figure out why, but I'm grateful."

Calloway indicated a bottle and a couple of glasses on a table nearby. "Better have a couple of stiff ones," he said. "You look like you need them."

McCord poured raw liquor into his stomach, and welcomed the bite of the vicious stuff.

"If I'm not mistaken," Calloway said, "you're the jasper who tried to throw down on Bill Queen in front of the hotel."

"That's right."

"And that's why you aren't hanging by your neck about now."

"I don't get it."

"I want Queen, too."

"Oh—I see."

"I thought you would." Calloway leaned back in his chair and put his big feet up on the table. "I won't beat around the bush," he said. "If you've got any brains, you know I'm here because I'm smart enough to get by with it, and for no other reason. It's a pretty good deal, and I don't want to get pushed out."

"Queen's trying to do that?"

"Not exactly. That is, not yet, but I'm smart enough to know that he will. I'm like a horsefly buzzing around Queen's ears. That's our relative size and strength. The only thing in my favor is that I've got brains and Queen hasn't. I can figure his course before he knows what it is himself. So I know he's going to have to put me out of business before long— know it before he does."

"That little act you put on out there will just about cinch your finish, won't it?"

Calloway considered this. "Maybe— maybe not. It all depends on which way the cat jumps."

"The cat?"

"Meaning you. I stuck my neck out— sure— but I did it on a

49

gamble. I'm betting you'll get Queen."

"Thanks for the vote of confidence."

"I figure a jasper who'll gun down five men in a dive like the Blue Madonna, is a jasper who's worth a bet. Anyhow, I'm staking my future on you. Otherwise, I'd be backed against the wall in a month, anyhow."

McCord dropped into a chair at the other side of the table. "Tell me about Bill Queen. What do you know about him?"

"A plenty bad one. He played the war back east for all it was worth. Joined the Union forces early and got caught up with stealing supplies. He was supposed to face a firing squad, but he escaped and then tried to join up with the South. They wouldn't have him.

"He owns the Blue Madonna, and spends his time raiding all over the west. Understand he got back from a trip up in Missouri and Kansas not long ago. Brought a girl back with him, I heard."

"I can tell you some more. Plenty more—"

Calloway shrugged. "I'm not interested. Why waste time. All I want to know is: Can you get Queen?"

"I fully intend to get Queen."

Calloway got to his feet. "Then start doing it. But you're on your own, son. If you miss the next time, I won't be able to do anything for you. In fact, I'm going to drop out of sight for a few days until this little affair blows over."

"I'm on my own," McCord agreed. "Thanks for what you've done for me so far."

"Don't thank me," Calloway said, a trifle coldly now. "I work for my own interests at all times. If you ever get in my way, I'll see you hung."

McCord grinned. "Thanks anyway," he said, and walked out into the street. He went carefully, his mind and hand poised for action. But no one was waiting for him. There were no roaring guns. He went down to the hotel.

Upstairs, he paused before Patricia's door; almost knocked, then changed his mind. A dew minutes later, he was bedded down in his own room, sound asleep.

He opened his eyes when the knock came—pushed them open

with effort—to find dawn coming in through the blinds. The knock was repeated. McCord got out of bed and pulled on his pants. He lit the lamp, picked up his gun from the stand, and called, "Come on in."

The door opened slowly—first a small crack, then wide enough to admit the slight body of Neal. The little man had all the manner of a small boy moving toward a jam closet. He entered the room, then turned his back on McCord in order to look up and down the hall before closing the door.

Inside finally, he came across the room and sat down on the bed beside McCord. Now, the latter saw that he had a pad of paper and a pencil in his hands. McCord watched curiously, noting the conspiratorial air about Neal, the tense, eager light in his expressive eyes.

Without further ceremony, Neal wrote swiftly on the pad: *You want to kill Queen?*

McCord blinked in surprise. "That's right."

Again Neal wrote on the pad: *Come with me. I'll show you how to do it.*

McCord's first reaction was one of suspicion. "I'll get Queen in my own way. I don't need any help."

Neal's face fell. He wrote feverishly: *You do need help. Believe me. I know.*

"How can you help me?"

I found out something so I went to Queen and made a deal. I agreed to turn you and Patricia over to him— to lure you out to Bob's adobe so all he'd have to do is come and get you.

McCord's face darkened. His hands reached toward Neal's throat. Then he controlled himself. "Go on with it. Write it down, and write fast, "he growled.

Neal's pencil flew over the pad: *I told him I'd do it for money—that I'd have you and Patricia tied up waiting for him. That's what he thinks, but you won't be tied up. He'll come all alone and you'll be waiting for him.*

Neal finished writing and looked—eagerly, pleadingly, at McCord while he read the words. McCord scowled, his mind racing, mulling the thing over in his mind. The distrust, however, was heavy and compelling.

51

"Why are you doing this? What reason do you have?" Sure that Neal was in league with Queen—somehow and for some reason— McCord wanted Queen so badly that he could not reject the idea immediately.

Never mind my reason. Just remember that you can't get Queen any other way. He knows you're after him and now he's got a dozen men waiting to kill you. This way you can get at him. He'll come alone to the place on the desert.

"He'll bring men with him," McCord said harshly. "Even if you are on the level, which I doubt, you've overlooked that point. It would be trap. We'd be like rats waiting for Queen to move in."

Neal smiled eagerly and shook his head as he wrote: *No. He'll come alone. He'll do that because he wants Patricia. He'll come alone so he can put his hands on her right then and there.*

McCord made his decision swiftly. It was based on the knowledge that Neal spoke the truth about McCord's inability to get at Queen any other way. This way, he could come to grips with the swine, trap or no trap.

"All right," he said. "I'll go with you, but Patricia stays here."

Neal shook his head violently, and wrote: *No. She's got to come with us. Queen's men will be watching when we leave town. If she isn't with us Queen won't come. At least, he won't come alone.*

McCord knew he should have refused. But, with the scheme deep in his mind, its impossibilities of success apparent, he was loath to turn it down. Suppose Neal really was on the level? Wouldn't it be as well to gamble that way as otherwise, so long as the whole thing was a gamble anyhow? And as to harm coming to Patricia, McCord wasn't greatly worried about that. Trap or no trap, there was his confidence in his own ability. When Queen advanced on the adobe, alone or otherwise, McCord would have a rifle in his hands and a .45 Colt at his side. That would be all he needed.

The balance was tipped by Patricia herself. A light knock and she was in the room dressed for a ride. "Neal told me we were going to Bob's place," she said. "The three of us. I'm ready, but why are we going?"

She has absolute confidence in Neal, McCord thought. Then, he realized he was wrong. The realization came as he looked into

Patricia's beautiful eyes. They were trained on him, not on Neal. And the confidence radiating from them was directed at himself, not the thin little mute.

For a moment, he looked at her silently. A gorgeous morsel she would make for the stalking, bestial Queen. Queen would strip her without mercy and turn her into the lost beaten thing Candy had become.

But, on the other hand, she was wonderful bait— the finest bait in the world to dangle before a shark like Queen.

"Yes," McCord said. "We're going to the adobe. I've got to meet a man there. Let's get going."

Neal brought the horses and they rode out of the still sleeping town, the hooves of their three animals making soft echoes in the street.

If Queen or his men were watching, they remained hidden. Apparently, no one saw them but a drunk lying on the boardwalk. He opened one eye as they passed. Then, he closed it and went back to sleep.

McCord's feeling as they approached the adobe was one of extreme tension. Just outside of rifle range, he commanded a halt. With a grim look in Neal's direction—a look promising dire payment for treachery--McCord went on alone.

He approached the adobe from an angle, which would give a gunman waiting inside the poorest possible shot. He dropped from his horse in the shelter on the wall and approached the doorway. There, he got set and leaped inside, gun ready. There was no one to dispute his way. A check on the shed revealed that it, too, was untenanted.

McCord waved a hand, bidding his two companions to come forward. As they approached, McCord stood scowling at the diminutive Neal. He couldn't figure the man. So far, there was every indication that he'd been sincere in this coup. But there were so many unanswered questions. So much to be explained.

They rode up side-by-side, Neal and Patricia. Still scowling, McCord stepped between the horses to help Patricia down. Maybe Neal was on the level, he admitted to himself.

Then, the sky fell on him. Swift unconsciousness—the oblivion he'd already experienced since he'd started his long trek toward the Nations.

He came to with a splitting head. He opened his eyes to find himself bound tight to a chair with turn after turn of thin, tough rope. With his first thought came the certainty that escape from the chair was impossible.

Now, his eyes cleared, to focus on other objects in the room. Patricia, bound as tightly as he himself to another chair. Her eyes were wide with wonder; stark fear was mirrored in her face.

Nearby, squatting down against a wall, was Neal. He kept his bright eyes trained steadily upon his prisoners. There was a slight smile on his face—a look of almost childish happiness, as though he were eliciting praise for what he'd done.

"Neal hit you," Patricia said in a dull stunned voice. "He knocked you unconscious when you reached up to help me. Then, he dragged me down from the horse and tied me up. I—I guess I was just too surprised to resist until it was too late. Then, he tied you up."

McCord stared at Neal and felt the red waves of rage rising within him—self; rage at Neal, of course, but more so at himself for his own gullibility and stupidity.

"I've talked to him," Patricia went on. "Begged and pleaded with him, but he just sits there and pays no attention."

"He's gone mad," McCord said. "It's a waste of time talking to anyone as far gone as he is." Then, he belied his own statement by directing words to the placid Neal. "Look— can't you visualize? I don't know what made you do this, but you certainly must be able to see what Queen will do to Patricia. And you can't want that to happen. Let her go. Get her out of here and leave me for Queen, if you must. Just get her back to town and safety."

Neal smiled up at the two with a vacuity of expression that made McCord's blood run cold. With a quick look at Patricia, McCord took desperate measures. Speaking clearly and without haste, he went into detail as to what Patricia's fate would be. Steeling himself to the girl's reaction to his raw words and frank statements, he saw the color flame into her face, saw the torturing embarrassment and sheer agony in her eyes as he spat out in detail the picture of what her fate was to be at the hands of Queen. Somehow, he had to break through the vacuum around Neal's mind. Somehow, he had to reach and sting Neal's chivalry and decency.

But it was no use. He listened to the details of what Queen would do to Patricia, seemed to be considering the portrait McCord painted of her naked, helpless, brutalized future. Then, he got to his feet, head cocked in a listening attitude.

McCord heard the sound, too. A horseman approaching. Then, heavy footsteps and Bill Queen strode into the room. After the briefest glance at McCord, he turned his lascivious eyes on the cringing Patricia. The eyes reflected perfectly his intentions toward her.

Then, he looked at McCord. "Seems like history repeats itself, McCord." He glanced smugly about the room. "Scenery's a little different, but everything else is the same."

Patricia's voice came—still flat, dull. "How did you make him do it? What did you give him that could turn him against me this way, after he's done so much for me?"

Queen motioned toward Neal with his head. "You mean him, honey?" The leering desperado laughed. "Why, it was his idea." His leer deepened, and he rubbed the thumb and a finger of one hand together. "Gold, honey. *Dinero*. Money. He sold you to me by the pound, so to speak." Then, with a nod toward McCord, "And he threw the Kansan in as sort of a bonus."

Queen threw back his head and laughed. His eyes, bright and feverish as they rested on Patricia, closed for a moment at the height of his mirth.

At that moment, Neal struck.

From a position slightly behind and to the left of Queen, he brought a short club, which he'd had concealed in his sleeve, over in a vicious arc. The club cracked against Queen's skull, bringing the man down without a word.

Then, as McCord and Patricia stared in amazement, Neal went truly mad. He changed in that brief instant to a drooling, eager animal. With surprising strength, he grabbed Queen by the shoulders and dragged him through the doorway into the kitchen. During this process, he seemed oblivious of the prisoners. He was in a world of his own—a world with only two occupants—himself and Bill Queen.

The next half an hour was to be stamped forever on the minds of McCord and Patricia Morley—a half hour crammed with such vivid horror as to be unforgettable. With the body of Queen beyond their view, they saw Neal flit past the doorway carrying another length of rope. Then, he too vanished.

But there were sounds: Neal's weird yammering, his crooning, wordless voice giving out a sort of mad, obscene lullaby as he went about whatever he was doing.

Then, Queen's roar of rage when his consciousness returned abruptly. But soon the rage and defiance were gone, giving place to a squall of pain overshot with Neal's high-pitched laughter.

From then on, it was starkly sickening; something inconceivable even in the wildest nightmare. Queen's deep voice roaring with pain, to pitch higher and higher as the sounds became those of a suffering wild animal rather than of a man.

Sickness, pure and unadulterated, was in Patricia's face as her eyes pleaded with McCord.

"It's no use," McCord said. "He's beyond us; beyond reason." Then more to drown out the hideous sounds with his own voice than to explain, he said, "It's easy to see the truth now. Queen was the man who mutilated Neal back in Georgia. Neal wanted Queen himself. No doubt, he spied on the adobe back at the way-station and took a shot at Queen. He missed, and you had to run for it.

"Then, when we got to Santa Blanca and Neal found his enemy so close, he really went mad with a thirst for vengeance. He knocked me down when I tried to kill Queen there in front of the hotel, because he wanted Queen for himself. Then, his mad mind came up with this idea and—well, it worked.

"It's—it's horrible," Patricia whispered. "I can't—"

"Don't blame him too much," McCord said. "Remember, he's not sane anymore. He's not the same man you knew and trusted."

The ghastly sounds from the kitchen had faded out now, and for a moment there was complete silence. Then, Neal appeared in the doorway. Again, he had changed. The madness seemed to have faded. He was carrying a knife in one hand— a knife gouged and dripping with blood. It fell to the floor as he stood looking at the trapped pair. Neal's eyes were empty now— dull and devoid of expression. He was a picture of sated desire—revenge carried to the ultimate—a weary, bewildered, beaten man. His revenge was on his lips, and the taste was of ashes.

Slowly, he picked McCord's .45 from where it had fallen to the floor. Then, looking vacantly about him, he saw and retrieved the horrible knife. Listlessly, he applied its edge to the cords binding Wate, then to those holding Patricia helpless.

This done, he turned and walked slowly from the room. After clearing themselves of bondage, McCord and Patricia rushed to the door of the adobe. Out beyond, in the sunlight, Neal was walking straight away into the desert.

Patricia called out, "Neal—Neal! Come back!"

At the sound, the unhappy man turned and stood motionless for a moment. Then, he quietly raised the gun to his head.

The sound of the shot and Patricia's scream mingled in the clear desert air. She flung herself into McCord's arms, and he led her slowly back into the adobe. "Don't look," he said, as they passed the ripped, slashed and mutilated body of Bill Queen. But the admonition was unnecessary. Patricia's face was buried against Wate's chest.

It seemed there had been enough drama here in the dessert, enough and overflowing. But there was to be still more. Five minutes later, there came again. The sound of an approaching horse. McCord left Patricia in the front room and came out to the door. He saw Candy Thompson, booted and clad for the saddle, approaching at a gallop.

She pulled her horse to a rearing halt, flung out of the saddle and ran to the adobe. Seeing McCord, her eyes filled with fear. "What happened?" she cried. "I heard about it, and came as fast as I could to stop him. What happened?"

"Don't go inside," McCord said gently. "Stay out here."

The fear deepened. Candy flung herself past him and into the kitchen. There, she stood frozen for what seemed an interminable time, staring down at the horrible thing on the floor.

McCord never knew what prompted him to put his hands on Candy.

Possibly some deep instinct of self-preservation. Anyhow, by the time she found words, he was holding her tight in his arms.

She tried to spin around. Her head turned, and she was staring with horror up into McCord's face. "You did this to him—you!"

Before he could answer, she had become a raging, fighting fury. In a way, she had gone insane, just as Neal had earlier. "You son of a bitch!" she screamed. "I'll kill you! I'll cut you to pieces just the way you did him!"

McCord's muscles reacted without command to hold her helpless—hold her there with her face, revealing sheer, naked hatred, a few inches from his own.

"Candy—for Gods sake, Candy! Wha's happened to you?"

"Happened?" she screamed back. "I met a man, that's all. A better man than you could be in a thousand years!"

"Candy!"

She wanted to kill him, and if that couldn't be done, to hurt him. "Yes— a man" she spat. "A half hour after Bill Queen carried me away from the grove that night, he sent his men on ahead and dragged me into some bushes. In there, I fought him tooth and nail for a long time." She smiled up into McCord's face, relishing the pain she saw there, deliberately forming each word into a knife to stab into his mind.

"We fought until he had me stripped naked, and he was bleeding where I'd bitten through his ear and his lips. We fought until I slipped away from him and started to run.

"But then, something happened. Just in one instant it happened, and I stopped because I knew I wanted him as much as he wanted me.

"So I went back," Candy screamed, "Do you understand that? I went back naked into his arms, because I suddenly realized I'd met a man. Not a wishy-washy country bumpkin that's got red ears and fell over his feet every time he asked me for a kiss. A real man, and we had each other there in the bushes while you were eating dirt back in the grove."

Candy saw how she was torturing Wate, and strove to push the goad in deeper: "When we were through and came out of those bushes, he hadn't conquered me— I'd conquered him. He was mine, do you understand? Mine- body and soul—and I was his."

The girl stopped talking from sheer lack of breath. Still held in McCord's iron grip, she was panting and glaring hatred up into his face.

"I didn't kill Queen," McCord said quietly. "I'd have killed him if I'd had the chance—sure—but not that way. Queen's past caught up with him. Once, he mutilated a man—cut his tongue out— and the man found him and arranged this trap with me as bait. He did this to Queen, and then killed himself. He lies dead out beyond the corral."

She was silent, staring into his face.

He said, "Candy, regardless of appearances, don't you know I couldn't do that to a man, no matter how much I hated him?"

Candy collapsed like a rag doll as all the hatred and tautness went out of her. She slipped from McCord's grasp and went to the floor where she sat huddled. There was a time of silence, broken only by her quiet weeping. Then she looked up. "Yes, Wate. I know that. I'm sorry. I went crazy. I'm sorry I hurt you—wanted to."

"But—that's the way it was?"

Candy nodded, dropping her eyes. "Yes—that's the way it was."

His voice was low, miserable: "But we can go back. We can start over—"

She was on her feet now, her hand on his, compassion in her voice as she smiled at him. "No, Wate— it's no good. I'm no good, and in a way, it's lucky you found it out. I've had a taste of the wild free life, and it's my life. I don't know where I'll end up, but I'll travel the road with my eyes open, and I'll have no regrets when I come to the end of it."

He was staring into her eyes, and a quick expression of knowing came upon his face. "It was you who saved my life back there by the creek. You were riding with Queen and Antonio, and you kept Queen from killing me and the others."

Candy nodded, gave him a small, swift smile. "I told you I'd...conquered Bill Queen. We searched the wagon to see if there was any gold, but I wouldn't let him kill anyone."

"He chased the wagon because Neal took a shot at him from the darkness at the way-station?"

"Somebody took a shot at him. It was the man who killed him."

McCord nodded.

"I didn't hear about what was going on here until after Bill left Santa Blanca. I got wind of it and came out here to stop him. I was too late."

"Yes—you were too late."

Candy turned slowly toward the door. "Goodbye, Wate," she said.

"Goodbye."

Then she was gone. Wate did not watch her ride away. He turned into the other room.

He never saw Candy Thompson again.

I'm going back," Wate said. "Back to Kansas. I'm not a gunman by hand or at heart. I'm a farmer. I belong in Kansas."

Patricia said, "You loved her a great deal, didn't you?"

"I don't know. I thought I did. Yes, I loved her."

"Do you still love her?"

"I don't know."

"May I ride with you—at least as far as Kansas?"

"Certainly. What are you going to do then?"

Patricia smiled serenely. "The same thing I'm going to start doing right now. Make you forget Candy Thompson."

She began by kissing him.   THE END

www.ingramcontent.com/pod-product-compliance
Lightning Source LLC
Chambersburg PA
CBHW020651130626
46552CB00003B/1504